AF321714

DRACO DORMIENS NUNQUAM TITILLANDUS

Harry Potter™

GRYFFINDOR
HOUSE PRIDE

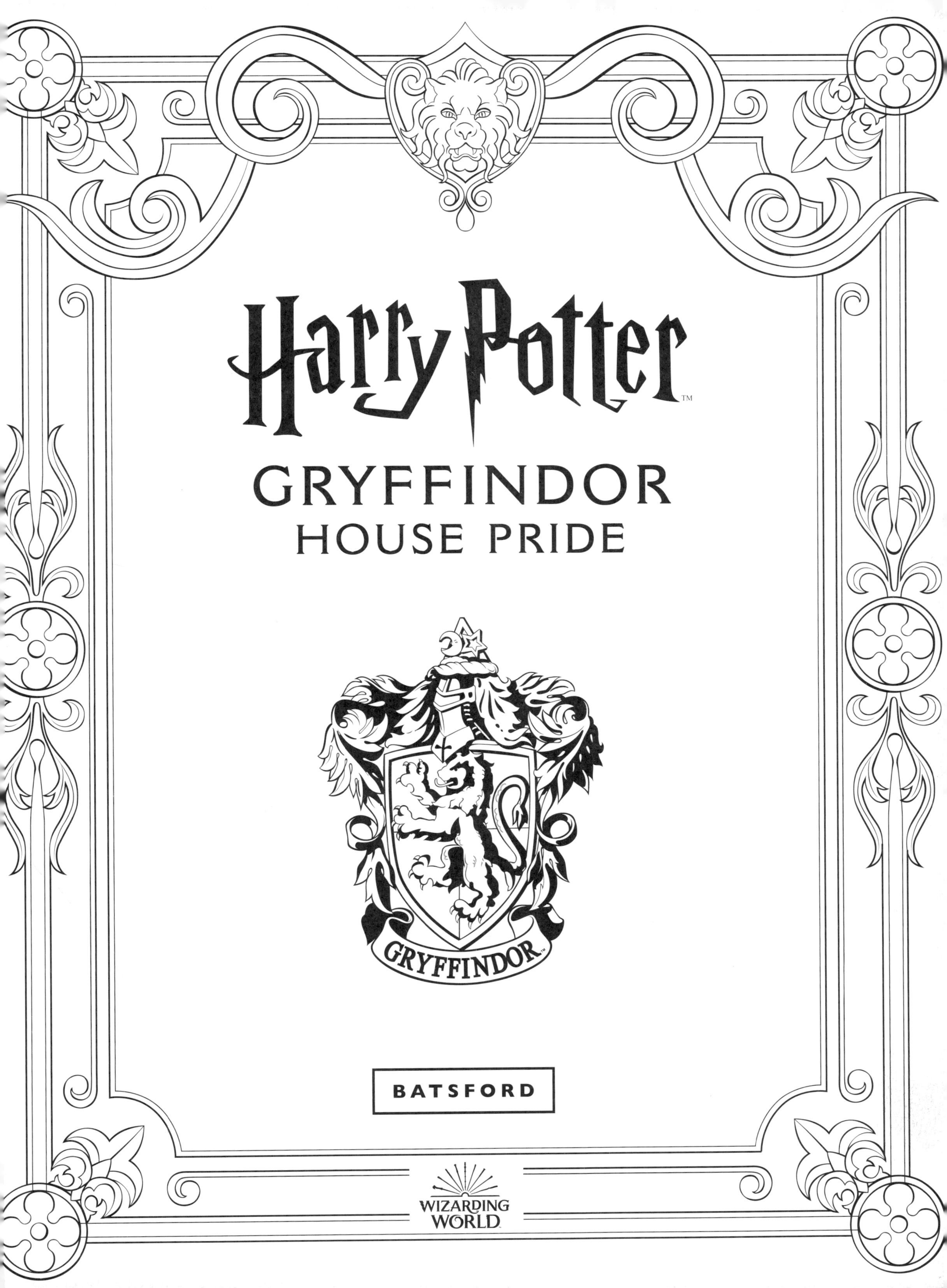

BATSFORD

GRYFFINDOR

FIZZING WHIZBEES
GLACIAL SNOW FLAKES
HONEYDUKES
EVERY FLAVOUR
BERTIE BOTT'S
BEANS
FIZZING WHIZBEES

Gryffindor

GODRIC GRYFFINDOR

7990 TD
7990 TD

DUMBLEDORE'S ARMY
H

131.5
Vol

First published in the United Kingdom in 2021 by
B. T. Batsford Ltd
43 Great Ormond Street
London
WC1N 3HZ

ISBN: 9781849947503

A CIP catalogue record for this book is available from the British Library.

10 9 8 7 6 5 4 3 2 1

Publisher: Raoul Goff
VP of Licensing and Partnerships: Vanessa Lopez
VP of Creative: Chrissy Kwasnik
VP of Manufacturing: Alix Nicholaeff
Editorial Director: Vicki Jaeger
Senior Editor: Greg Solano
Design Support: Megan Sinaed-Harris and Monique Narboneta
Associate Editor: Anna Wostenberg
Senior Production Editor: Elaine Ou
Senior Production Manager: Greg Steffen
Senior Production Manager, Subsidiary Rights: Lina s Palma

Thanks to all our artists: Remie Geoffroi, Maxime LeBrun, Pablo Matamoros,
Hend_draw from Fiverr, Tomato Farm, Conor Buckley, Paula Hanback, and Iván Fernández Silva

B. T. Batsford Ltd, in association with Roots of Peace, will plant two trees for each tree used in the manufacturing of this
book. Roots of Peace is an internationally renowned humanitarian organization dedicated to eradicating land mines
worldwide and converting war-torn lands into productive farms and wildlife habitats. Roots of Peace will plant two million
fruit and nut trees in Afghanistan and provide farmers there with the skills and support necessary for sustainable land use.

Manufactured in China by Insight Editions